Books By Rick Bentsen

The Blademaster Chronicles
The Blademaster
Willowdale
The Age of Darkness
** Dragonsbane

The Blademaster Chronicles Boxed Sets
^ The Beginning

The Legacy of the Blademasters
The Legend of Raven Windrider
** The First Blademaster

The Chronicles of Xarin
The Crucible

Gamma Strike
+* Dawn of a New Age
The Dawning of a New Age

The Chocolate Sheriff

+ Out of print
* Released through iUniverse
** Forthcoming
^ eBook only

THE CHOCOLATE SHERIFF

BY RICK BENTSEN

Steel Drake Press
Boston

The Chocolate Sheriff

For information, contact the author at
rickbentsen@rickbentsen.com

www.rickbentsen.com
www.facebook.com/RickBentsenAuthor

This is a work of fiction. Names, characters, places and incidences are the product of the author's imagination. Any resemblance to actual locales or people or events is purely coincidental unless otherwise noted in the acknowledgements.

FOREWARD

July 17, 2016

My name is Johnathan Chalmers. This book is my story. When my friend Jenny introduced me to Rick Bentsen, I had no idea that this would mean one of my stories would finally see print.

What I had no idea was that it would not be just any story, but MY story. Every word you are about to read is true. This really happened. And I am thrilled that Rick was able to capture all of the important details.

I hope you enjoy my story. Now that my name is in print, maybe I will have the courage to finish a book of my own.

I guess we will just have to see.

I want to thank Rick for taking this book seriously. He has told my story better than I could.

I also want to thank Lucy... you'll meet her shortly... for her part in this story. We were married last month.

I can't tell you how happy I am that this special woman has become my wife. What she has done for the kids we serve at Camp Aldridge... Well, when you read this book, you'll understand.

Please, enjoy the story. And if you're ever in the area, please make sure you are careful. I can't promise that all of the unquiet spirits in the area have left.

The Chocolate Sheriff

You just never know who's hanging around still.

-Johnathan Chalmers
The Chocolate Sheriff
Camp Aldridge

ACKNOWLEDGEMENTS

I have often said that writing a book is not a process that one can do by himself. The actual writing is a solitary process, but there are the people you bounce the ideas off of, the people who edit for you, the people who tell you whether or not the book is good. And each of those people is very important to the writing process.

Consider this, as usual, to be a free pass. You don't have to read these thank yous if you don't want to, but these people deserve to have their name in print.

Thanks to my parents and my brother for their unconditional love and support. And for believing in me when I didn't completely believe in myself.

Thanks to my friend Jenny for introducing me to Johnathan Chalmers.

To Johnathan Chalmers and Lucy McCullors for letting me tell you their story.

To my editor, Joanna of Elliott Editing, for all the amazing work she does to make sure I don't sound like a blathering idiot in my books.

To my significant other and my children, thank you for the support and for the belief in me. Especially when I felt like giving up.

Finally, thanks to the fans, without whom there would be no point in my continuing this dream of becoming a writer. Keep reading! I'll keep writing!

The Chocolate Sheriff

Rick Bentsen

*This book is dedicated to
my daughter, Kaitlyn.
You amaze me every day.*

The Chocolate Sheriff

THE CHOCOLATE SHERIFF

DRAMATIS PERSONAE

Johnathan Chalmers, The Chocolate Sheriff
Lucy McCullors, owner of Camp Aldridge

Camp Staff:
Libbie Saunders, proprietor of the General Store
Sally Macadam, seamstress
William Forsythe, Banker
Clive Saunders, Weaponsmith and
gun/archercy range supervisor (Husband to
Libbie Saunders)
Roger Westbrook, Inn/Housing proprietor
Tim Murdoch, Head Chef
Albert Westin, Saloon owner
Penny Westin, Piano player and singer
Thomas Albert, Barber
Roger Braddock, Stagecoach owner
Jimmy Ward, Stagecoach driver

Campers:
Sadie
Jade
Christopher
Amy
Tommy
Bobbie Jo
Eugene
Carmen
Carlos
Alonzo

John Red Crow, old Apache shaman

The Chocolate Sheriff

PROLOGUE

Greetings, Faithful Readers!

You know, as I travel around the world promoting my books, people tell me stories. I suppose that it is only human nature that people want their stories told, after all. Most of these stories never make it into one of my books, but I love hearing people's stories anyway. Most of the time, the stories I get told are so outrageous that there's no way I could incorporate the story into one of my books. And, considering I craft fantasy stories for a living, that says a lot. Still, occasionally I get told a story that is so good and so right for me that I have no choice but make sure that the story gets told.

The book you are about to read is one such story.

The story came about on a trip to Arizona. I'd gone out there for a promotional event for The Blademaster. An old friend of mine came up to me with this guy in tow. The guy was wearing an Old West sheriff's outfit, complete with a .44 Colt revolver. I had no idea what to make of this.

"Rick," my friend said to me. "This is Johnathan Chalmers. I want you to hear his story. I think you'll like it. I think it would make a great plot for one of your books."

Ok. I will admit that this intrigued me.

So I took this Johnathan Chalmers fellow aside and had him tell his story briefly. I had to admit that I did not believe him at first. When you read what happened, I am sure you will see why. Still, the tale piqued my interest. It was just such a crazy enough tale that there was no way that it could be true.

Still, as I said, I was intrigued. And I was intrigued enough to check the story he told me out. I was amazed at what I found out.

Everything he told me had happened just as he told me it had!

Like me, Johnathan Chalmers was an author. But, unlike me, he had never been able to finish a book, let alone get one published. He had read The Blademaster, and he enjoyed my writing style. He told me that, even though I wrote in the fantasy genre, he felt that I could tell his story far better than if he tried to write it himself.

Once I checked out his story and found it to be true, I sat down with Johnathan and his fiancée, Lucy McCullors, so that I could get all of the details of the story down correctly. After all, if I was going to tell this story, I wanted to do right by him and tell the tale just as it happened. I wanted to know everything that he was thinking and feeling as it happened.

Since I was going to finally have this man have one of his stories told to the world, I wanted to make sure it was a good one.

So, the three of us sat up late in my hotel room one night eating bad Chinese food and talking about the tale. Little by little, I got the entire story out of him. It was a lovely evening, to be honest, and I would like to think I got two lifetime friends out of the deal. Johnathan (never John or Johnny) was an engaging storyteller, which made me wonder why he could never finish one of his own books. And Lucy chimed in where she could to help round the tale out.

By the end of the night, I had the full story of how Johnathan Chalmers became the Chocolate Sheriff.

And as with any good tale involving an author, it all started with a rejection letter...

The Chocolate Sheriff

CHAPTER 1

ohnathan Chalmers was 29 years old, and, as of yet, had not figured out what he wanted to do with the rest of his life. He had flitted from one job to the next over the years, but nothing took. It was frustrating to him that he could not figure out his true purpose in life.

And so, he had turned to writing.

So late at night, he would sit in front of an old Royal Safari typewriter and try to write the next Great American Novel. He had finally figured out something that he was passionate about.

The only problem was that he just had nothing to say.

And then one night after a long day of serving people coffee, he finally struck on an idea that he thought might make for a good story. It was the start of a space opera series. It told the story of a vast Star League that covered most of this part of the galaxy. He wasn't completely sure how good he would be at writing science fiction, but he threw himself into the writing. A week after he came up with the idea, he had written three chapters along with a synopsis for the rest of the book.

He made a copy of everything and sent it all off to Star Wind Books, hoping that the publisher would like the story enough to pick it up.

As he waited for the response from Star Wind Books, Johnathan tried to finish up the rest of the manuscript with the thought that, should they accept the book, he should have the full manuscript ready to send to them.

Unfortunately, after that first bit of writing, he wrote very little of the rest of his book. Oh, it was true that he knew what he wanted to say. But he was having a very hard time getting the story from his brain onto the written page.

He struggled for weeks trying to get more written, but most nights, he simply stared at the blank page in his typewriter. On a really good night, he might get a couple sentences written. Most nights, though, he did not even get that much done.

Three months after sending off the first three chapters of the book off to the publisher, he had managed to get just two more chapters written.

He figured that, at that pace, it would take him several years to finish writing the book. All he could do was to keep plugging away at his typewriter every day and hope that he got the inspiration he needed in order to finish the book in time.

But his lack of progress frustrated him to no end.

And so it was that he was not in the best frame of mind when he finally did get a response to his submission from Star Wind Books.

It had been a long shift at Dunkin Donuts. A lot of people had come in, and there had been more than a couple of mixups on orders throughout the day. All that Johnathan wanted to do was to go home and take a nap. Probably a shower first, though, to get the coffee and donut smell off of him. The last thing that he wanted to do was to sit in front of the typewriter and work on his book.

The Dunkin Donuts he worked at was about a 10 minute walk from where he lived, which was great for him as he chose not to have the expense of a car. Being able to walk back and forth to work meant that not having a car was much easier.

Girls, of course, did not like that he did not drive, however. It had been the nail in the coffin of more than one relationship. He dreaded hearing another woman say, "I'm sorry, but I just can't date someone who doesn't drive." Most of the time, Johnathan did not care about the state of his love life. Or lack thereof. But every now and then, he did get lonely.

The apartment that he lived in was on the first floor of a house that had been converted into apartments. His apartment was in the back of the house. There was a door at the back of his house that led to his apartment. He loved his little apartment. It was a one bedroom apartment, but it had a small extra room that he had converted into his writing room.

As he did every day when he got home from work, Johnathan went up the front stairs to where the mailboxes for all the tenants in the building were. He grabbed his mail without looking at it and went inside the building to his apartment. He dropped the mail on the dining room table and turned the overhead light on. He checked the phone to see there were no messages, and then he went in to take a shower.

Only after his shower did Johnathan look through his mail.

He threw all of the bills into one pile and threw out the junk mail. And then there was, at the bottom of the stack of mail, a letter from Star Wind Books. With shaking hands, he slit open the envelope and pulled out the single sheet of paper.

Mr. Chalmers,

After carefully reviewing your submission of "The Star League," we have come to the editorial decision that we cannot accept your manuscript at this time. We feel that the story, while good, is very raw and requires a great deal of work before publication.

In addition, you have indicated that the manuscript is not yet complete. It is not our policy to accept manuscripts that have not been completed. Please note, then, that this is not a final rejection of your work, but merely a summary rejection of an unfinished project.

There is also some concern that the characters and plot in your book appear to be somewhat derivative. While we are, in no way, calling your creativity into question, it would be a poor business practice to accept a manuscript that appeared to be a derivative work of other published works as this appears to be. It would open us, as the publisher, and you, as the author, to potential legal action.

We do see great potential in your work. We encourage you to finish the manuscript and resubmit. If you can address our concerns, then we may yet choose to publish this work.

I wish you the best of luck in your continued writing endeavors.

Sincerely,
Rachel Winters
Acquisitions Director
Star Wind Books

Johnathan reread the words on the page several times before putting the letter down. He went over to his liquor cabinet and pulled out a fifth of Stolichnaya vodka. After filling a glass with ice, he poured himself a generous drink and picked up the letter again. He read it over again as he sipped his vodka. As he read the letter again, he could feel his aspirations as a novelist going up in smoke. It was true that they told him that they welcome to resubmit the book once it was finished.

It was just that now he was not sure it would ever be finished.

As the night wore on, he refilled his glass several times as he thought about his options. Johnathan was not much of a drinker normally, but that night, as he felt his dreams crumbling around him, he finished the entire bottle of vodka.

When he went to pour himself another glass and found the bottle empty, he groaned and set his glass down on the table. He walked into his writing room where his desk was and put the rejection letter in the center drawer. There was little else he could do, so he simply went to bed early. He had had no supper, and he had done no writing. He was simply done with the day.

And, for the first time since he was ten years old, Johnathan Chalmers cried himself to sleep.

CHAPTER 2

The next morning, Johnathan woke with a massive headache. He knew he had drunk too much the night before, and he was paying for it now.

He stumbled to the kitchen and winced as he turned on the overhead light. Coffee. That was what he needed. He filled up the pot and measured out the grounds. Once everything was set, he started the brewing process and began the interminable wait for the coffee to finish. When it did, he poured himself a cup and took a big sip.

Sighing happily, he sat at his desk. The half finished manuscript sat on his desk, mocking him. He picked up the manuscript and slid it into a drawer of the desk, where he knew he would probably forget about it. He had known from the moment he read the rejection letter that he probably would not finish that manuscript. He was still sure that he had a book in him to be told, though.

Johnathan was back to square one, though, as far as what to write. They had been right that the story he had tried to tell had been very derivative of other space opera stories that had already been written. And while he loved science fiction, he began to doubt that his writing talents actually fell into that genre. Maybe that was his problem. Maybe he needed to look into trying to write in a different genre. He knew that whatever he wrote needed to be character driven. His favorite part of writing so far had been to create the various characters that he would write about.

He took out a pad of paper and a pen and started to doodle. It was his way of tapping into the ether that all authors tapped into. He would doodle on the pad until something came to his head. He had no way of knowing what that something would be, though.

Maybe he would try his hand at a Western. That was a thought. Create an Old West gunfighter that travelled around looking for adventure. That could be fun. He would have to read a bunch of Westerns in order to get the feel of things for that genre. That was fine, though. He loved to read, and any excuse to go to the library became something worth doing.

He finished his coffee and poured himself another cup while he thought about the possibility of writing a Western. He did not know much about being a gunfighter. Johnathan had not fired a gun since his days in Scout camp. He would have to do some research on the weapons of the Old West and figure things out from there. It definitely meant a trip to the library. While he was there, he could check out some Western books. Maybe some Longarm or The Gunsmith books. He'd always enjoyed reading those during various parts of his life anyway.

Johnathan got up from the desk and made his way into the bedroom to get dressed. He chose a simple black T-shirt and black jeans. The T-shirt actually had no design on it, for a change. A Boston Red Sox cap and a pair of sneakers quickly joined the attire chosen. He grabbed his keys and was out the door.

The walk from his apartment to the library was not a long one, but it was long enough for Johnathan to clear his head somewhat. By the time he got to the library, the fog of his hangover had lifted, and he was thinking clearly. He hummed softly to himself as he climbed the stairs to the entrance of the library. Now that he had a plan of action, he knew that he would be able to put the rejection letter in his past. He would learn his lesson from the mistakes he had made with that story and go forward with a renewed confidence in his abilities.

It was all he could do.

He did not know what drove him to look at the newspapers, but after he collected some reference materials on guns of the Old West and a few Western novels, he found himself looking through classified ads. While he was happy working at Dunkin' Donuts and enjoyed being able to so conveniently get his coffee fix on work days, he knew that it was not a job that would truly help him advance his career as a writer. He needed something new and different.

He needed an adventure.

He had given thought to leaving New England, even, but he did not have any idea about where he would go if he were to leave Massachusetts. He knew, though, that his story was out there somewhere. Somewhere away from where he grew up.

He just had to find it.

As he scanned the classifieds, he hoped he knew what it was that he was looking for when he found it. Most of the jobs that were listed were simple office or manual labor jobs. He knew that those were not what he was looking for. It wasn't esoteric enough to be able to give him the adventure he was craving in his life.

Near the end of the classifieds was a small ad that caught his attention. Of all of the ads in the paper, it was the only one that really called to him and felt like what he was looking for.

WANTED:
Individual wanted for position at Old West themed camp for underprivileged children. Must

be willing to relocate to the camp for the position. If interested, call Lucy McCullors.

There was a phone number on the ad. A quick check on his phone told Johnathan that the phone number was from Arizona.

He made a photocopy of the ad and then checked out his books.

While he wasn't positive, he believed that he had found what he was looking for. He would call this Lucy McCullors. And if the job was actually what he was looking for, he knew that he was one step closer to finding his story once and for all.

The Chocolate Sheriff

CHAPTER 3

ohnathan was excited about the prospect of working at an Old West themed camp. He knew that it would help his creative process. It also served as an indication that maybe, just maybe, he had found his writing niche after all.

But he was nervous. This would be a huge change for him. And there was also the fact that he would have to talk to this Lucy McCullors person. He pictured her as this little old lady. It was the picture he had to have of her if he was going to be able to make the phone call in the first place.

Johnathan had little confidence when it came to women.

It wasn't that he did not like women. To be fair, he probably liked women too much. He was a Scorpio and had the Scorpio's libido, after all. But he had no confidence when it came to talking to them. He had not had a girlfriend in close to two years as a result. And so, even though he was calling for a job and not for a date, he was still nervous.

He wandered into the kitchen and poured himself another cup of coffee to steel his nerves. As he took a sip of his coffee, he thought about the job. The ad had not said what the job at the camp would be. He was, in essence, applying for a job blind. He had no idea if he had the qualifications needed for the job. The thought actually excited him a little bit. Not knowing what the job would be made the prospect of the job much more interesting.

He took his coffee into the living room and picked up the copy of the ad. When he looked at his cell phone, he saw that it was late enough to be a reasonable time to call someone on the West Coast.

No time like the present then, he thought.

Johnathan took another swig from his coffee before dialing the number on the ad. Taking a deep breath, he hit the SEND button on his phone.

The voice that answered his call did not sound like it came from a little old lady, but Johnathan kept that picture firmly in his head when he talked to her.

"Camp Aldridge. This is Lucy McCullors speaking," the voice said when she answered. "How may I help you?"

"Miss McCullors, my name is Johnathan Chalmers. I'm calling about an ad you ran in my local paper about a job at your camp."

"Ah, yes," she said. He could almost hear her smile. "Yes, we are looking to fill that position as soon as we can."

"Well, I am certainly interested in learning more about the position, and, perhaps, applying for it."

"Wonderful!" Lucy said. "I see that you are calling from Massachusetts. I will actually be out there next week to interview a perspective camper. Maybe we can meet for coffee, and I can explain about the camp and about the job."

"That would be great. I guess you can call me on this number when you're ready to meet for coffee."

"I will do so," Lucy laughed. Her laugh was like the tinkle of wind chimes. "I look forward to meeting you, Mr. Chalmers."

"I am looking forward to it too." As he hung up the phone, he realized he meant it.

But he also began to wonder just what it was that he had gotten himself into.

The Chocolate Sheriff

CHAPTER 4

 ohnathan did not give his meeting with Lucy McCullors any thought over the next week. He spent the time either at work or reading for research for the book he planned to write. And so it was, that when she called that Thursday morning, it caught him by surprise.

He had just poured himself a second cup of coffee and was sitting down with a book about guns of the Old West when his phone rang.

"Hello?" he said after pressing the answer button.

"Mr. Chalmers, this is Lucy McCullors. We spoke last week about a job opening at my camp that you were interested in."

"Yes, I remember," he nodded, even though he knew she could not see him. "You had said you wanted to meet in person when you were in the area."

"That's right," she said. "If you can suggest a good place near you where we could get sandwiches and coffee, I'll break for lunch and we can discuss the job opportunity."

"How about Café Resco on Main Street in Taunton?" he suggested. "There's a parking lot just off Main Street where you can park for free. It's a short walk there for me. What time should I meet you?"

"I'll be finished with this intake interview by noon," she said. "Meet at the café around 1?"

"That works for me. Should I bring anything?"

"Just yourself. And an ID and Social Security card if you accept the job offer. I have new hire paperwork with me in case you do."

"OK," he said. "I'll see you then."

After hanging up with Lucy, Johnathan slumped back on his couch. He was not sure he was ready to actually meet this Lucy McCullors. He did not have a choice, though. He had agreed to meet her. He had to follow through.

He had a bit of time before he had to go over to the café. Shrugging, he went in to grab a quick shower. When he was done, he sat down at his desk and looked over his notes for the book he wanted to write. Things were starting to come together in his mind as far as the main character. He had decided that the main character for the story would be a deputy US

36

Marshal named Colton Webster. He'd put Colton in the Denver office right around the time that Colorado became a state. All he had to do was to flesh out the character and then come up with a good story to tell for the first book. He envisioned that this could be a fairly lengthy series of books.

He kept a close eye on the time, and soon enough, it was time to leave if he was going to be on time to meet Lucy McCullors.

It was not a far walk from Johnathan's apartment to Café Resco. He felt a little bad about having Lucy come so close to where he was living for their meeting, but he did not have a hard time rationalizing it to himself. Since she was from out of town, he supposed that it really did not matter where they met.

He made sure that he had everything that he needed and locked the door behind him. He started humming to himself as he made his way down the road towards Main Street and Café Resco.

It was a beautiful day and the sun was shining. Being late spring, it still wasn't too hot. It was a little humid, though, and he knew a rain storm was probably coming soon. There were clouds on the horizon, but they were far enough away that he was comfortable thinking that he would be able to get back to his apartment before the rain started.

He might even have a new job by the time he got home.

When he got to Café Resco, he looked through the window. There was no one in the café save for the girl behind the counter. When he checked the time on his phone, he saw that he was still about ten minutes early for his meeting. It was rare for him to be early for something, but he guessed it would make a good first impression if he were there before his potential boss. So he went in and ordered himself a café mocha.

"I'm meeting someone," he said. "I guess I'm a little early, though."

"Okay," the girl said as she turned to make his mocha. "Since you're a paying customer, I guess it's all right if you sit and wait."

He nodded and waited at the counter. When she came back with his café mocha, he paid for it and went to sit at one of the small tables looking out over the street. He took out his notebook and started to work on a character study for the deputy US Marshal he had decided on for the Western books. He liked to handwrite character studies like this. It had always allowed him to feel closer to his characters. He had always felt that the characters were the key to any story. And, by extension, doing the work to make sure that the characters were complete and fleshed our characters made for a better story.

He was so engrossed in what he was doing that he never heard the door to the café open. So he was very surprised when the young woman that entered the café walked over to the table he was sitting at and cleared her throat.

"Excuse me," she said. "Are you Johnathan Chalmers?"

"I am," he said, looking up. "Miss McCullors?"

"Lucy, please," she smiled. "I am happy to meet you."

Lucy McCullors was not what he had pictured in his mind. She was definitely not a little old lady like he had pictured. She was much closer to his age, likely even a year or two younger than he was. She had long, curly, flame red hair, which was more than enough to get Johnathan's undivided attention. He had always had a thing for redheads. And she had the pale milky white skin that suggested the red hair she had was all natural. She was cute, and definitely a woman that he could easily become attracted to.

Which could also present a problem if she became his boss.

"Please, sit," he smiled back. "Can I get you a sandwich and a cup of coffee?"

"There's no need to pay for my lunch," Lucy said, the smile spreading slightly. He decided he really liked her smile.

"Miss Lucy, you may very well be offering me a job today. The least I can do is buy your lunch as a token of my gratitude."

"Do they have egg salad?" she asked.

"Yes, and it is a particularly tasty one," he said.

"Very well. Then I will have an egg salad sandwich and a coffee," she nodded. "Cream and sugar, please."

"As you wish," he bowed slightly.

He went over to the counter and placed her order. He tried not to think about how he had just quoted his favorite movie. More than that, he tried not to think about the implications of what he'd just said. He was not normally one to believe in love at first sight, but there was something about this Lucy McCullors that could maybe bring out the hopeless romantic in him.

It did not take long for the girl behind the counter to finish making the sandwiches and coffees. He paid and brought the food back over to the table. Lucy threw another smile his way.

And with that smile, he knew he was in deep trouble.

Before she started to tell him about the job he was applying for, she took a bite of her sandwich. Her eyes closed and she moaned softly in pleasure. Johnathan was happy that the sandwich met with her approval. The moan of pleasure did little to avert his nerves, though.

"So," he said after a bite of his own sandwich. "Tell me about Camp Aldridge."

"Camp Aldridge is, as you know, a camp in Arizona," Lucy began to explain. "We are a camp based on the Old West. The camp is set up as an Old West town, in fact, complete with inns, a saloon, a gunsmith. Everything you'd find in an Old West town except for a whorehouse, since that wouldn't be all that appropriate for a kids camp.

"Our campers are underprivileged kids who would otherwise not be able to go to a camp. Three weeks out of every month, we have anywhere from fifteen to one hundred campers.

Most months, we are closer to a hundred campers. Parents pay nothing for their kids to attend the camp, not even airfare. All of the money we need comes from donations and grants."

"That's an amazing idea," Johnathan said.

"Thank you," she smiled again. "It is very rewarding to be able to give kids an experience like this. I have always wanted to do something like this. When the opportunity to purchase Camp Aldridge came up, I took it."

"And what would my job be at the camp if I were to take the position offered?" he asked.

"My sheriff has recently retired," Lucy said. "He served the camp well, but he was getting on in years and he decided to hang up his badge. I'm offering you his position."

"I have to tell you, I don't know anything about being a sheriff, Miss Lucy," he shrugged. "I can't even begin to guess what kind of a sheriff I would make."

"You would receive some training on police procedures in Phoenix if you take the job," she said. "I would make sure you were not unprepared for the position."

"I would need to give two week's notice at my current job," he said. "And it will take me some time to pack up my belongings."

"If you're accepting the position, we'll try you out for three months. I'll pay for a storage unit here for you for those three months until you are sure about whether or not you're going to stay on full time. Are we agreed?"

"Well, Miss Lucy," he said after taking a sip of his coffee. "I believe you have yourself a new sheriff."

CHAPTER 5

The two weeks leading up to his move to Arizona were very busy for Johnathan. He spent much of his daytime hours packing up his apartment. He was amazed as to how much stuff he had accumulated over the years. Since he was not sure how much room he would have in his living quarters at the camp, most of his belongings would be going into the storage area that Lucy had agreed to pay for.

He placed his belongings neatly into boxes, separating them into piles of boxes that were going to Camp Aldridge and boxes that were going into storage. He would have the belongings going to the camp shipped out the week before he left for Arizona.

At night, his thoughts were all about her.

He could not put Lucy McCullors from his thoughts. No matter how hard he tried, he could not stop thinking about her. He did not know nearly enough about his new boss. He did not even know if Miss Lucy was single or not.

Johnathan figured that would be something he would need to find out quickly about Lucy McCullors if he was going to pursue a romantic relationship with her. And he was sure that he wanted to pursue such a relationship with the fetching redhead.

He wondered how she would feel about that.

He hoped that she would feel the same way as he did in time. He was in no hurry, though. For the time being, he would just enjoy his new job.

The more he thought about it, the more excited he was about the idea of working at a camp for underprivileged children. He could understand why Miss Lucy was so passionate about her camp. It was a good thing to be able to do something good for kids who did not have much, and it was something that he found himself looking forward to being a part of.

A week before he was ready to fly out, he shipped several boxes to the camp. He shipped boxes of books that he could not bear to be without as well as his typewriter and his notebooks full of notes that he had made for his various writing projects. He had called ahead, and Lucy had assured him that his boxes would be waiting for him in his living quarters when he arrived.

The day before he was scheduled to fly out, the truck came to take his belongings to the storage facility that the camp was paying for a locker for. Lucy had said she'd pay for three months of storage while he decided whether or not he wanted to stay on at the camp. After that, he would make other arrangements for those belongings.

It felt odd to see his apartment completely empty. He had not seen it in such a state since the day he moved in four years previous. He would miss his apartment, although he would not miss some of his neighbors. Most notably, he would not miss the annoying older woman that had been living above him for the previous year and a half. She had caused him no end of aggravation, and she blamed him for all of her troubles, even though he had actually been the cause of none of them. As much as he loved his apartment, he would not miss hearing her out in the hallway outside of his door calling for her cat at all hours of the day and night.

He wasn't sure if moving out to the desert was the best way to resolve his annoying neighbor situation, but he was happy that it was a definite positive side effect of the move.

The day of the move came quickly enough. When he awoke that morning, he packed up his travel bag and took one last look around his apartment. It felt odd to be leaving the apartment that had been his home for the previous four years, but he knew that he was doing the right thing. His future finally had a direction and he was looking forward to exploring it. And he was looking forward to spending time with Lucy McCullors. The more he looked at the situation, the more he decided that he had made the right decision by taking the job. Even if it did mean he was moving to the other side of the country on a whim.

He would learn to love the desert as much as he had come to love New England.

He gathered up his travel bag and called his landlord to go over the apartment.

When his landlord got to the apartment, Johnathan stood in the living room while she went through the apartment inspecting it for damage. She was thorough, and it took her almost a full hour to finish inspecting the apartment.

"Well, everything looks to be in order," she said as she came back out to the living room. "Not that I expected anything different from you."

"I tried to keep it in the same condition as I got it," he shrugged. "Perhaps there's a little wear and tear, but..."

"Are you sure I can't change your mind about leaving, Johnathan?" she asked. "You have been such a model tenant, and we really hate to lose you."

"I know, Deb," he nodded. And then he smiled a broad and bright smile. "But the opportunity I have been given is far too good an opportunity to pass up."

"Well, in that case, I shall wish you the best of luck," she smiled a sad smile at him. "If you ever come back this way, please come by and let us know how you're doing."

"Of course," he nodded again.

She handed him a check for his security deposit, took his keys, gave him a hug and left.

There was nothing left for Johnathan to do but to head to the airport.

The Chocolate Sheriff

CHAPTER 6

It was an uneventful flight from Boston to Phoenix. Johnathan really did not like flying. He had a real fear of heights and traveling in a skinny tube of metal that had nothing but wind below it made him sick to his stomach.

But, aside from losing his lunch halfway through the flight, the skinny tube of metal got him to Phoenix unharmed.

He was looking a little green when he stepped off the plane, but his color quickly returned to normal once his two feet stepped onto solid ground. He slung his carryon over his shoulder and went off in search of the baggage claim.

Phoenix was a larger airport, but the signs telling people where to go were very clear. So all he had to do was follow the signs to baggage claim. He made his way through the airport to the baggage claim, hoping that all of his bags would actually be on the carousel. He had the fear that he would get to Phoenix, but none of his belongings would.

When he got to the baggage claim, he found the carousel where his bags were supposed to be. He waited with others from his flight, watching for the conveyor belt to start spewing out suitcases. When the suitcases started coming out on the conveyor belt, everyone except Johnathan rushed up to grab theirs. He waited, knowing that his bags would still be there when everyone else was gone if they were there at all.

People slowly started clearing out from beside the conveyor belt. When there was space enough for him to get in comfortably, Johnathan moved in and started watching for his four bags. He'd had to pay extra to be able to bring four suitcases, but since he did not think he would be returning to Massachusetts, he figured he needed to just bring all of his clothes anyway.

It did not take long for his bags to show up, and he breathed a sigh of relief when he saw them. The last thing he wanted to do was start a new job without anything to wear!

He put his bags on a trolley and started to make his way towards the exit.

"Johnathan Chalmers!" he heard someone call. He recognized the voice as Lucy McCullors.

The camp director herself had come to pick him up from the airport! "Over here!"

He looked around and caught sight of her flame red hair. Once he'd sighted on her hair, he threaded his way through the crowd, dragging his trolley behind him. It took a bit to get to her, but soon he was standing in front of his new boss.

"Miss Lucy," he nodded once. "As you can see, I made it."

"You did, indeed," she smiled. "Come. There's a car waiting to take us to the depot."

Johnathan nodded and she led him through the crowd of people to the exit. When they got outside, she led him over to a car. She helped him load his luggage in the trunk. She got in the passenger seat and he took the backseat behind the driver.

"Tim, take us to the Camp Aldridge depot," Lucy said. She turned to face Johnathan. "The stagecoach will take us the rest of the way to the camp. We like to immerse the kids in the feel of the Old West from the very start, so it's a stagecoach ride through the desert to get to the camp."

"A stagecoach ride?" he asked. "How fitting."

Lucy smiled at him before turning back to look out the front windshield.

They rode in silence through the streets of Phoenix until they got to the outskirts of town. At the far east edge of town, they came to a small building that could only be a stagecoach station. While he had never seen one, he had read enough Westerns to recognize it for what it was.

They pulled into a small parking lot behind the building and climbed out of the car. They pulled his luggage from the trunk and went inside.

"Greetings, Miss Lucy," an old man behind the ticket counter said. "Ready to go back to the camp?"

"Sure am, Roger," she nodded. She pointed at Johnathan. "This is Johnathan Chalmers. He's our new Sheriff."

"Welcome, Sheriff Johnathan," the old man smiled a gap-toothed smile at him. "I'm Roger Braddock. I run the stage coach from Phoenix to Camp Aldridge. Jimmy Ward will be your driver today. He'll take good care of you."

"Thank you," Johnathan nodded. He was starting to feel slightly overwhelmed, and he knew it would get worse when he began to meet all of his new coworkers at the camp.

Lucy led the way out to where the stagecoach was waiting for them. Johnathan followed quietly, carrying all four of his bags carefully. It was quite the balancing act to carry all four bags at once. He would have liked to have had a trolley to carry them, but he understood that the experience of the Old West had started as soon as he had walked into the station.

He understood why Lucy had chosen to start the experience at that point for the kids.

When they got out to the stagecoach, the driver helped him load his bags into the storage area in the back of the coach.

"Miss Lucy, the horses are watered and we're ready to go whenever you are," the driver said. "If you and your companion would like to get in, we'll be underway."

"Thanks, Jimmy," Lucy flashed him a quick smile.

Jimmy opened the stagecoach door and Johnathan moved forward to help Lucy up into the coach. She smiled at the gesture and let her help him. He climbed up into the stage behind her and sat on the bench opposite from her.

He knew it would be presumptuous to sit next to her.

The ride from Phoenix to Camp Aldridge took just over three hours by stagecoach. Johnathan was sure that if he were to just ride a horse from the camp to the city, it would take far less time. But with the added weight of the coach, the horses could not move as fast.

Of course, the thought of just riding a horse from the camp to Phoenix was a silly one. Johnathan had never ridden a horse in his life and wasn't sure he would be able to. He suspected, though, that it was just one more thing he would learn in his time at the camp.

He watched the desert landscape go past the coach. He wasn't sure he'd remember how to get from the camp to the city with no landmarks, but he figured he wouldn't have to do so by himself any time in the near future. And by the time he would actually have to, he would have learned the way.

They did not talk during the ride. Johnathan was content to watch out the window. Lucy alternated between watching him and watching out the window herself. He could feel her looking at him from time to time, but he did not turn to meet her gaze.

He was afraid he might not be able to turn away again.

When the coach pulled up to the station at the camp, Johnathan got out of the coach first so that he could help Lucy down. The driver helped Johnathan collect his bags from the back of the coach.

Johnathan followed Lucy across the gravel parking lot of the stagecoach station. There was a wooden bridge over a small stream that Lucy was leading him towards. On the other side of the stream, Johnathan could see Camp Aldridge.

They crossed over the bridge, and Johnathan started to look at his new home for the first time. The camp was arrayed like a small Old West town, although it was a bit larger than most. The roads were dirt, and the buildings on both side had boardwalks in front of them. There were hitching posts in front of the major buildings. Johnathan could make out a saloon, a couple shops, a bank, and several inns.

And, of course, the sheriff's office.

Lucy headed straight for the sheriff's office. Johnathan followed close behind.

"I thought we'd stop at your office first," she said. "Your living quarters are actually above the sheriff's office. I thought you'd want to stash your bags before meeting the rest of the staff."

"Very thoughtful," he nodded.

Lucy led the way into the sheriff's office. His office now. When he walked through the doors, he was amazed at just how much the office looked like it had come straight out of one of the Western books he loved to read. There was a desk, which he assumed was his desk. Old faded wanted posters lined one wall. There were some small cells in the back. And there was a door near the cells. When he opened it, he saw that there was a set of stairs going up. He figured that was the way to his living quarters. He dragged his bags up the stairs and looked around.

The apartment was smaller than his apartment in Massachusetts had been, but it would be big enough for his purposes. There was a small desk in the living area that had already been set up with his typewriter and his notebooks. He did not really like that someone had been through his boxes to set the apartment up for him, but he was willing to overlook it.

"I apologize," Lucy said from behind him. "I should have let you unpack your boxes, but I wanted the room to feel like it was yours when you got here. So I unpacked your typewriter and your notebooks for you. Don't worry, I didn't look through anything."

"It's okay," he said. "I was just surprised to see my things out already. I think I'll be comfortable here."

"I hope so," Lucy smiled. "Now that I've hired a new sheriff, I'd like to not have to hire another one anytime soon."

"I don't think you're going to have to," he said. "But as you said, I have three months to decide."

He left unsaid that he probably would stay even if he hated it if it meant being able to stay close to Lucy.

"When you're ready, come downstairs and I'll introduce you to the other members of the Camp Aldridge staff. They're all looking forward to meeting the new sheriff."

CHAPTER 7

e spent a few more minutes looking around his new apartment before locking the door with the key that Lucy had given him. He went back downstairs to where Lucy was waiting for him by his desk.

"Ready to go?" she asked.

Johnathan nodded. He was feeling a little overwhelmed at everything that had happened since landing in Phoenix. The feeling would pass, he knew, but for the moment, it was what he was feeling.

Lucy pushed the doors open and led the way down the boardwalk to the general store. She pointed out the saloon with its batwing doors, the barber, the bank, a small café, and the inns where the campers slept.

Johnathan was amazed at just how well Camp Aldridge had been put together to resemble an Old West town. It was as if he had been transported back in time to the days of gunfighters and gamblers.

He loved it.

When they got to the general store, Lucy led the way inside. The store was much like Johnathan had expected it to look. There were all manner of supplies on shelves and tables. It was not a large store, but it was fitting with the theme of the camp.

Behind the counter was a slightly plump young blonde woman. Her hair was very curly and she was wearing a plain blue dress. She smiled at Lucy and waved her over to the counter.

"This is Libbie Saunders," Lucy said by way of introduction. "She runs the general store. She also hands out the mail when it comes."

"Miss Libbie," Johnathan nodded slightly at the shop owner.

"Libbie, this is our new sheriff, Johnathan Chalmers."

"Very pleased to meet you, Sheriff," Libbie beamed at him. "But we're going to need to get you some more appropriate clothes. Sally will be able to help you look the part." She turned and called to a tall black haired woman that was looking at some supplies. "Oh, Sally! We have a young man in need of your talents."

The black haired woman turned and smiled at Lucy. She looked Johnathan over from head to foot, making him feel like he was being inspected. She tapped her fingers against her chin, thinking about what she could do for him. Finally, she nodded.

"I think I have some things that will work for you, Sheriff," Sally said. Clearly she had overheard the introduction. "The jeans will work fine. I have some good Western shirts that I think will be a good fit for you. And a nice black Justin hat, I think."

"Thanks, I think," Johnathan blushed at the attention.

"And boots. You'll need boots," Sally frowned at his sneakers. "What size show do you wear?"

"12."

"I have a pair that should fit you then," Sally nodded. "You seem to like black, so these will work nicely for you."

Johnathan looked over at Lucy who was clearly amused by the exchange.

"You need to look the part if you're going to work here, Johnathan," Lucy reminded him. "Sally's the best seamstress around. We're lucky she agreed to sign on to the camp. She'll get you set up appropriately."

"This is all quite overwhelming," he said softly.

"Oh, everything will calm down soon," Lucy laughed. "Everyone is just excited to meet you.

"Clive will want to get Sheriff Johnathan set up with an appropriate gun, Lucy," Libbie said. "He'll have a gunbelt for him too."

"I haven't shot a gun in years," Johnathan grimaced. "I don't think I'm a good shot."

"Don't worry about that, Sheriff," Libbie laughed. "My Clive will make you a crack shot in no time!"

"Well, I certainly hope so," Johnathan grunted.

"One last thing, Sheriff," Lucy said to him. He turned to see she was holding something out to him. "This is yours. You should get used to wearing it."

Johnathan took the pin from Lucy. It was a brass six pointed star with the word SHERIFF etched across it. He could feel the heft of the pin. And he knew that it would feel a little heavier when he was wearing it on his chest.

"I guess you're right, Miss Lucy," Johnathan nodded. "This badge is mine to wear now, I should start wearing it."

CHAPTER 8

ver the next month, Johnathan was kept very busy. For that first month at the camp, he actually spent very little time at the camp and interacting with campers. Most of his days were spent in Phoenix learning police procedures at the Phoenix Police Department Headquarters. There was a lot for him to learn, and he took his studies seriously.

At night, he would sit in his quarters at the camp and struggle with his typewriter.

He had all of the research he could possibly want for his story, but he did not make any progress on his story during that first month. He blamed it on being tired from all of his studies. He did make some small progress on plotting out the story, though, so at least he felt like he had made some progress.

He had missed an entire session of campers, though. He had not so much as said hi to a single camper during that first month. It bothered him a little, even though he knew that he was doing what he had to do in order to be able to do his job in the future.

And he had hit on an idea as to how he could win the campers over when he started to interact with them during the next month. He'd get Libbie at the general store to hook him up with chocolate that he could carry around and give to the campers.

Chocolate always made children happy.

When the Police Department was ready to sign off on his training, he brought that paperwork to Lucy. She was happy to see how hard he had worked and put the paperwork in his file.

She was pleased that he had completed his training.

"You'll greet the next group of campers when they arrive," she told him.

"OK," he nodded.

And that was that.

He had a week to get ready before he had to greet the next group of campers. During that week, he spent a lot of time on the gun range practicing with the Colt .45 that Clive Saunders had presented him as the Sheriff. Clive had taught him how to take care of the pistol as well as how to shoot it accurately. While he was not the best shot ever, he could generally hit the target with every shot.

The week leading up to when the new set of campers were going to arrive went quickly. Johnathan established a routine for doing rounds around the camp. He walked the camp in the morning, stopping in at the general store for the mail and for any rumors that might be going around that he needed to know about. Libbie was only too happy to pass around any gossip that she'd heard.

He would then spend a couple hours in his office doing paperwork, when he had paperwork to do, and generally just giving the appearance that there was a sheriff in the sheriff's office. Then he would do another walk around the camp in the afternoon.

During that afternoon walk, he would stop at the gun and archery range and spend a little time practicing with his pistol or practicing with a bow and arrow. Clive had suggested that he spend time familiarizing himself with the bow and arrow as well as the pistol. And so he had decided to spend time practicing both. Old memories of shooting a bow at his old Scout camp as a kid came back to him. He was happy to see that the arrows at Camp Aldridge were well care for and flew straight.

The morning that the campers were to arrive dawned bright. It had started to get to the warmer part of the year, but the location of the camp was such that there were mountain breezes that blew through the city helping to cool it down a bit compared to the surrounding desert.

Johnathan made his morning rounds, knowing that the campers would not arrive until early afternoon. When he stopped off at the general store, Libbie waved him over with a smile.

"New campers today!" she exclaimed. "This is always a fun day."

"My first new camper day," Johnathan smiled. "I'm looking forward to it."

"You seem to be settling in well," Libbie said. "Clive says you've been taking well to his lessons."

"Clive knows more about guns than anyone I've ever met," Johnathan laughed. He slapped his hand on the counter. "I'd be foolish to not take advantage of such knowledge."

"Well, he likes you," Libbie said. "I heard him give his stamp of approval to Lucy. That's some high praise."

"I hope to never let him down, then," Johnathan nodded. "I suspect I wouldn't like to be on his bad side."

"No, I suspect you wouldn't," Libbie winked. She leaned forward. "But don't worry. It takes an awful lot to actually land on Clive's bad side."

"Good." He looked around the store before leaning closer. "Have you given any thought to what I asked you about earlier in the week?"

"Why, Sheriff, of course I have," the store owner nodded. "I will happily provide you with chocolate to bribe the children."

"It's not a bribe!"

"It's a bribe," Libbie laughed. "But it's a sweet bribe. I think it's a wonderful gesture. I think you're going to do well here, Sheriff."

"I hope so," he smiled. "I like it here. I like the people."

"You like the Lucy," Libbie teased.

"Is it that obvious?"

"To anyone that has eyes, yes," she laughed. "We've all seen the way you look at her."

"Have I made a fool of myself?"

"No, you haven't," Libbie said. "But perhaps you should just ask her out. I think it would do you both good."

"I'll think about it," he grunted. Johnathan took a peek at his pocket watch, which was just another thing he had had to get used to as far as changes while working in the camp. When he noted the time, he sighed. "I guess I best be off. The coach will be here soon and I need to be at the station when it gets here."

"Think about what I said, Sheriff," Libbie said. She leaned forward and whispered, "I bet she'll say yes if you ask."

He rolled his eyes as he made his way out of the general store.

The camp had more than just the one stagecoach, he soon learned. There were several. He realized he should have realized that long before now, as it was how the campers arrived at the camp. There was nowhere near enough room in one coach for a hundred campers, after all.

When he crossed the bridge from the camp to the gravel of the stagecoach lot, he could see five coaches coming in. He'd timed his arrival perfectly. He stood at the end of the bridge and waited for the coaches to come to a stop.

The drivers of each of the coaches dropped down from the driver's seat and opened the doors to their coach. The campers filed out of the coaches and formed lines next to each coach. The drivers pulled the campers' luggage from the back of the coaches and called each camper's name for them to collect their bags.

When all the campers had their luggage, the drivers guided them over to where Johnathan was standing, waiting for the campers.

Johnathan looked over the campers, counting nineteen campers. He had known it was going to be a month with fewer campers this month. He was happy for that, as he wasn't sure he was ready for a month with one hundred campers.

"Greetings, campers!" he said in a bright voice. "My name is Sheriff Johnathan Chalmers, and I want to welcome you all to Camp Aldridge. How many of you have been here before?"

Every one of the campers raised their hands. This made Johnathan breathe a sigh of relief. He wouldn't have to explain everything to new campers.

"Here you go, Sheriff," one of the drivers said as he handed Johnathan a sheaf of papers. "Here's the list of all the campers that arrived."

"Thanks," Johnathan nodded. He looked over the list and over the campers. "If you'll follow me, I will get you all settled."

As they started across the bridge, Johnathan caught movement out of the corner of his eyes. He whirled to the side on the middle of the bridge, his hand dropping down to his gun, but he did not draw. He thought he saw an old man for just a moment, but whatever it was he saw disappeared quickly.

He couldn't be sure he hadn't imagined it.

Frowning, he turned back towards the camp and led the campers to their housing assignments. But he did not forget about what he thought he'd seen, and he filed it away for future reference.

The Chocolate Sheriff

CHAPTER 9

he next morning, Johnathan got up and did his normal morning rounds. He made his way around the camp talking to all the other staffers. It was a pleasant morning, and he'd almost forgotten about the weird sighing from the day before. He hadn't forgotten, but he'd filed it away.

At the café, he stopped for a quick bite of breakfast. He was surprised to see Lucy sitting there sipping coffee. He didn't have time to sit and have a long conversation, but he walked over to her table after grabbing a cup of coffee.

"Morning, Miss Lucy," he smiled at her. "Good morning, Sheriff," she smiled back. "It's a lovely day. Thanks for bringing the campers in yesterday."

"No trouble at all," he nodded. He started to turn but stopped, remembering what Libbie had said to him the day before. "Miss Lucy, I was thinking."

"That seems to be potentially dangerous," her smile widened. "What were you thinking about?"

"I was thinking... Er, would you have dinner with me on Friday night?" He could feel the blush starting to burn his face.

"I would love to, Sheriff," she nodded. "Swing by my house around 5 and we'll have dinner here, if that's all right?"

"That would be lovely," he nodded. He looked over at the counter and saw his breakfast was ready to go. "If you'll excuse me, Miss Lucy, I have rounds to finish."

"Of course, Sheriff. I'm looking forward to hearing all about your first week at our date on Friday evening."

She'd called it a date. Johnathan wasn't sure if that made him more or less nervous. He touched the brim of his hat and gathered up his breakfast, feeling like it would be better to get out of the café before he said or did anything stupid.

When he got to the range, he waited until Clive waved him to come on the range before he made his way to where he was teaching a group of campers. It was a simple safety matter to wait until the range master said it was safe to enter.

It was easy to be accidentally shot if you just barged onto the range.

The campers all seemed happy to see him, even though he knew most of them were not comfortable with a new staff member just yet. He had a pocket full of chocolate bars that he hoped might sway them a little.

Bobbie Jo, a 10 year old girl, was standing at the line with a bow in her hand. He watched as she pulled back on the string and let fly with her arrow. It did not go anywhere near the target as she yanked the bow back when she released.

Clive started to walk over to her, but stopped when Johnathan walked over and knelt beside her. Johnathan saw the range master hide a smile behind his hand at the sheriff kneeling down to help the little girl.

"Here, Bobbie Jo, is it?" Johnathan said softly.

Bobbie Jo nodded and handed the bow to Johnathan.

The sheriff took the bow and put Bobbie Jo's hand at the right spot on the bow itself. He put the arrow on the string for her.

"Now, hold your fingers like this," he said, imitating how he wanted her to hold her fingers. "Just like that. Then put the arrow between the first two fingers of your hand against the string."

She had trouble figuring out what he meant, so he gently took the bow and showed her what he meant. He curved the first three fingers of his right hand and gently grasped the nock of the arrow between the first two fingers. He showed her how to use those three fingers to pull back the string.

"When you loose, you want to let all three fingers go at once like this," he said.

He pulled the string back, aimed and loosed the arrow. The arrow zipped away to hit the target. Not quite a bullseye, but it was a good shot nonetheless.

He gave the bow back to Bobbie Jo, and she did her best to copy what Johnathan did. This time, her arrow actually hit the target, albeit the outer ring of the target.

"I did it!" she squealed with happiness. "I hit the target! Thank you, Sheriff!"

She wrapped her arms around his neck and gave him a hug. It was a moment that made taking the job worth it. He wrapped his arms around her and hugged her back. When she pulled away from him, he reached into his vest and pulled out a Milky Way.

"Here," he smiled. "Since you did such a good job."

She took the candy and ran over to where the rest of the campers were sitting.

Johnathan stood up and walked over to Clive and looked at the other man, who was failing at hiding his amusement.

"What?" Johnathan asked.

"You are enjoying your job way too much, young man," Clive laughed.

"Well, if you're going to do a job like this, you should enjoy it," Johnathan said. He turned back to look at Bobbie Jo. "Besides. The hug she just gave me was worth every candy bar I could ever give out."

"I'd say you just made a positive impression on one of our campers," Clive nodded. "I wager she'll be following you around in no time."

"Well, if she does..." Johnathan trailed off, frowning.

"What is it?" Clive asked, looking at what Johnathan was looking at.

"Wait here," Johnathan said softly as he pulled his pistol free. "Keep an eye on the kids."

Johnathan jogged off the range and around to where he thought he had seen the old man again. When he got to the spot where he thought he had seen the old man, he found slightly matted grasses, but no other evidence that anyone else had been there.

He holstered his gun and went back to the range. Clive looked concerned as he came back over.

"What did you see, Sheriff?"

"There was someone out there watching the range," Johnathan said. "I saw him yesterday when I brought the kids in from the coach. I could swear whoever it is was watching me."

"What did you see when you got there?"

"Just some matted grasses," Johnathan shrugged. "Couldn't even see where whoever it was had gotten in."

"I will help keep an eye out for you, Sheriff," Clive nodded. "Things like this make me a little nervous when they happen here. These kids are our lives here, you know."

"I know," Johnathan smiled. "Believe me. I do know that."

He clapped Clive on the shoulder and continued on with his rounds.

CHAPTER 10

he week flew by.

Johnathan spent much of the week walking around the camp and having fun interacting with the campers. He had become known as the Chocolate Sheriff amongst the campers because he had developed a penchant for slipping candy bars to the campers. One camper, Bobbie Jo, he knew had a peanut allergy, so he made sure that when he slipped her a candy bar, it was a Milky Way. He made sure she wouldn't be hurt by his kindness.

The campers quickly accepted him. And not just because he gave them chocolates. He always had a smile for them and made sure that they felt welcome and special at the camp.

Lucy had noticed the way that the campers had embraced the new sheriff, and it made her happy. It also made her far more inclined to accept when Johnathan had asked her for a date. She had appreciated how he had embraced the concept of the camp and how he had gone to great lengths to make sure the campers had an experience they would never forget.

She was sure she had hired the right man for the job.

On Friday, Johnathan finished his rounds by stopping at the general store. He wanted to pick up some flowers for his date with Lucy. It never hurt to make a positive first impression on a date with some flowers. It almost always helped to make his date smile, although, since he hadn't had a date in years, he wasn't sure it was still the surefire thing it had always used to be.

When he got to the general store, Libbie smiled at him when he walked in. She always seemed happy to see him. But from what he could tell, Libbie was happy to see everyone. She was just a naturally happy girl.

"What can I do for you today, Sheriff?" she asked when he got to the counter.

"Flowers," he said. "I need flowers."

"Yes, so I heard," Libbie grinned. "You have a big date tonight."

"Yeeeeeees," he said slowly. "I do. Did she tell everyone?"

"Just a couple of the girls," she winked. "We talk, you know. She was happy you asked."

"Well, that's good to know," he blushed.

"Aww, don't blush!" Libbie laughed. "You'll do fine. I have a nice bunch of carnations here for you. She loves carnations. There's an important tip for you. Carnations are her favorite flower."

"That..." he stopped and looked at her. "That is actually very good information. Thank you."

"You're welcome, Sheriff," she nodded. "Just remember one thing. If you hurt her, there will be a public lynching. And I'll lead the lynching."

"I don't think that's likely to be a problem," he said. "I don't have all that much luck. It's just as likely she friend zones me."

"Just be your normal charming self and you'll be fine, Sheriff."

"As you say," he nodded.

He took the bouquet of carnations and went out of the general store. It wasn't a long walk to Lucy's house, and it was a lovely evening, so he figured they could walk to the café.

He was in a good mood, and he hoped that nothing would happen to spoil the date. Something was nagging at him though. The mysterious appearances of the old man that had been happening all week had been bothering him. He wished he knew who the old man was and why he was checking Johnathan out.

Because he was sure by now that that was what the old man was doing.

For some reason, Johnathan had caught this old man's interest. He wanted to know why. What did this old Native American want with Johnathan?

It was a problem to figure out another day. This day, all he was concerned about was enjoying his first date with Lucy McCullors.

When he got to Lucy's house, he knocked on her front door. He did not wait long for her to answer.

She smiled at him when she opened the door. Her smile widened when she saw the carnations he was holding.

"Miss Lucy," he touched the brim of his hat. "These flowers are for you."

"Why thank you, Sheriff!" she said. "They're lovely. Carnations are my favorite."

She took the flowers from him and went back into the house long enough to put the flowers in a vase. When she came back out, she had a straw sun hat on.

"Shall we go?" he asked.

He offered her his arm, which she took. He had decided that if he was going to be the sheriff of an Old West camp, then he should display the manners of a gentleman. It was not a far departure from his normal nature, though. He'd always been the type to hold doors open for ladies and things like that.

But it was nice to see such acts were appreciated by Lucy.

They walked slowly down to the main street where they stepped on the boardwalk. They passed the general store on the way to the café and Johnathan could swear he saw Libbie give him a thumbs up on their way by.

When they got to the café, the chef, Tim Murdoch, met them at the door. He smiled at Lucy and nodded slightly to Johnathan.

"Sheriff, Miss Lucy, we have a table by the window for you," Tim said. "Miss Lucy, can I assume you're going to have your usual?"

"Of course, Tim," Lucy smiled. She looked over at Johnathan. "Tim makes an excellent steak."

"I can't argue with an excellent steak," Johnathan smiled. "Especially if it comes with a nice fluffy baked potato."

"Sounds like Sheriff Johnathan will have my usual as well, Tim," Lucy chuckled.

Tim nodded and brought them over to the table by the window.

They sat and chatted about the camp and the campers. They simply clicked, and Johnathan did not feel nervous talking to Lucy at all. Something he was very surprised by.

When the steaks came out, Johnathan took a bite and moaned in appreciation.

"Now that is just a perfect steak," he sighed happily.

"Told you," Lucy laughed.

"You did indeed," he said after another bite. "That might be the best steak I've ever had."

"So," she said, deciding to switch the conversation. "I have a favor to ask you, Sheriff."

"Oh, boy," he grunted. "What can I do for you, Miss Lucy?"

"You know we're doing a campfire tomorrow night, right?"

"Yes, I am aware," he nodded. He took a bite of potato and chewed thoughtfully. "What of it?"

"I've heard a rumor that you sing."

"I've been known to from time to time," he nodded. "I'm not very good though."

"Perform for the kids at the campfire," she said. She interlaced her fingers and rested her chin on her hands. She gazed at him from that position. "For me."

"Not sure the songs I know are appropriate for a campfire, Miss Lucy," he said after a moment. "I know a bunch of songs that the Highwaymen did, but most of them involve a lot of outlaw type things."

"That's all right," she nodded. "Pick the one you think you'd be most comfortable doing. I think it would be a good experience for you."

"All right, I'll..." He trailed off when he caught sight of movement on the other side of the street.

When he looked closer, he saw it was the old man he'd been seeing all week long. He stood and started towards the door, but by the time he got to the door, the old man was gone.

He went back to the table and sat back down.

"What was it?" Lucy asked.

"There's this old man that I've been seeing all week long," Johnathan frowned. "I swear he's checking me out. Every time I notice him, by the time I start to go confront him, he disappears."

"An old Native American man?" Lucy asked.

"That's the way he looks, yeah," he nodded.

"Sounds like John Red Crow," Lucy frowned. "He's an Apache shaman that leaves near the camp. He almost never comes into town, though. If he is checking you out, there must be a reason. I am sure you'll find out what it is soon."

"Sorry to interrupt dinner by bolting off like that," he said as he picked his fork back up again.

"It's all right," she smiled at him. "You're developing sheriff instincts. I'd much rather you investigate when you feel like something is wrong rather than letting it go and having there be a problem in my camp. Even if it means abandoning me at the supper table."

"I'll try not to abandon you at the table in the future," he nodded. "Thanks for indulging me, though."

"Of course."

They finished dinner with no more talk about mysterious old Native American men. Even though it was much on his mind.

The Chocolate Sheriff

CHAPTER 11

The next morning, Johnathan groaned when he woke up. He remembered the promise he made Lucy to perform at the campfire. He did not know what had made him agree, other than the fact that he could not disappoint Lucy. Or the campers. But mostly Lucy.

He had borrowed a guitar from Penny Westin the night before so that he could practice, but he did not know what songs he should practice. As he had said to Lucy the night before, a lot of the songs he knew were not necessarily appropriate for 9 and 10 year olds. But he decided that, since it was an Old West camp, a song about outlaws would be appropriate for the campfire. He settled on Silver Stallion by the Highwaymen, which was one of his favorite songs.

And he decided he would tack on a second song to practice as well. He remembered a song about the Concord stagecoach that he'd heard years before, and he decided to practice that one too.

He knew that that one would surprise Lucy.

Instead of going for his rounds, Johnathan spent the day in his little apartment above the sheriff's office practicing the two songs. He wasn't entirely comfortable performing in front of a crowd, but, by the time it was time to head over to the campfire, he knew the two songs well enough that he would be fine.

The campfire was held just outside the camp. They'd build a little area where they could safely have a nice big fire without having to worry about it burning down any of the buildings in the camp. They'd felled and set logs as benches in a semi-circle around the fire pit, and Clive had built a stage to the side of the fire pit that the various skits and songs could be performed on.

When Johnathan arrived at the campfire site, he saw that most of the campers and camp staff had already arrived. Lucy waved him over to where she was sitting. She'd saved a seat right next to her for him. He smiled as he made his way over to her.

He put the guitar down and sat.

"I see you're ready to perform tonight," she smiled when she saw the guitar.

"Yes, I have two songs ready for tonight," he nodded. "I'm not crazy about doing this, but a promise is a promise."

"And you did promise!"

When the rest of the campers arrived, Lucy walked over to the stage and turned to face the campers and staff.

"Well, we're here for another fun campfire," she smiled out at her campers. "This is, quite honestly, my favorite night of each session. And not just because there are s'mores for everyone!"

The campers laughed at that. Johnathan appreciated that there would be s'mores. What was a campfire without s'mores after all?

"Tonight, we will have lots of fun skits," Lucy continued. "And our very own Sheriff Johnathan Chalmers has agreed to do not one but two songs for us this evening." Johnathan blushed at that. "And so, without further ado, let's start the fire!"

Lucy waved and walked back to her seat. She patted Johnathan's knee and smiled at him.

"So now what?" he asked.

"Now, we watch as the fire gets lit in the only way we do so here at Camp Aldridge," she said. "Watch!"

The fire pit had been built up into what would be a large bonfire, perfect for this kind of campfire. Johnathan watched the pile of logs and sticks, not knowing what he should expect. Suddenly, out of nowhere, a flaming arrow streaked through the air, landing perfectly at the bottom of the pile of sticks, igniting the kindling there. Soon, there was a roaring bonfire going in the fire pit.

"Clive," Johnathan said. "Only Clive could make that shot."

"He enjoys showing off like that," Lucy laughed.

They sat and watched as the campers put on several fun skits. Some of the campers did little songs. Soon, the time came for Johnathan to do his two songs. It would close out the campfire.

Lucy gently pushed his back telling him to get up and get singing. He walked over to the stage and hopped up on it so that he was sitting on the edge.

"Miss Lucy made me agree to sing tonight," he said. "I'm not very good, so bear with me." The campers giggled. "I have two songs. The first is a song that was done by the Highwaymen a few years back. I find it appropriate since the horse Miss Lucy gave me to ride when I'm working is a beautiful silver stallion."

As he launched into the song, he watched Lucy's face. When he got to the part about finding a reckless woman, she smiled. He wondered what she was thinking. When he finished the song, though, the campers gave him a rousing round of applause. It made him feel better about his performance that they enjoyed it.

He adjusted the cap on the guitar's neck for the next song.

"I'm going to give you guys a little history lesson for this one," he said. "You all know the beautiful stage coaches that bring you in to camp when you come? Those are called Concord coaches. They were made by the Abbot Downing Company in New Hampshire, and they became the reason that we were able to spread from coast to coast in the times of the Old West. Most people know that part of the story."

He cast a glance at Lucy, and he could tell that she was wondering where he was going with this.

"What a lot of people don't know, though, is that, when Lewis Downing helped design the Concord coach, he did it out of love for his wife Lucy." Another quick glance over to Lucy saw she was smiling slightly. "I heard a song a number of years ago that stuck with me about their story."

As he launched into the song, he watched Lucy's face. She smiled broadly at him and closed her eyes as she listened to the beautiful love story of Lewis Downing and Lucy Wheelock. It was a beautiful song, and he did his best to sing it well.

When he was done, he hopped off the stage and walked back over to his seat and sat back down, leaning the guitar against his thigh. Lucy leaned against him, letting him know without words how much she appreciated what he had done.

Clive stood and told everyone it was time to head back to the camp. He turned to the fire and started to knock it down so that it could be put out completely.

Lucy slipped her arm around Johnathan's as they started back to the camp. She did not say anything to him, but he could tell that the song he'd sung about Lucy Wheelock had moved her.

He did not see the old man watching them walk back to the camp.

CHAPTER 12

fter the campfire, Johnathan walked Lucy back to her house. She was content to let him. It was a pleasant night for a walk, and he enjoyed having her on his arm. When they got back to her house, she gave his arm a squeeze before pulling away.

"Would you like to come in for a cup of tea, Sheriff?" she asked.

"I'd love to, Miss Lucy," he said. "But I best not. It's getting late, and I should be getting to bed soon."

"Well, then," she said. She sounded a touch sad that he declined her invitation. "Thank you for tonight, Johnathan. It was lovely of you to do those two songs for the campfire."

"I did promise," he smiled.

"You did, indeed," she smiled back. She leaned up and touched her lips to his. "And you were very good."

He blushed at her praise. He still did not think he was a very good singer, but he was glad that she enjoyed his performance anyway.

"The kids certainly seemed to enjoy the songs," he said. "I think more the first one than the second one."

"I liked them both," Lucy said, keeping her arms wrapped around him. "I felt like you were singing that second song right to me."

"I guess in a way I was," he said. "I can't lie to you, Miss Lucy. I believe I might be developing feelings for you."

She leaned up and whispered one word in his ear. "Good."

With that, she pulled away and walked into her house. He was left hoping she meant what he thought she did by saying "Good" to him like that.

Sighing, he went off to return the guitar he'd borrowed and head to bed.

When he got back to his apartment, he was still thinking about what Lucy said to him. It was becoming clear that she did share his feelings. That made him far more comfortable about expressing them. It also made him very happy.

He looked at the typewriter sitting on his desk and thought that he should type for a while. He'd been feeling somewhat more motivated to write lately even though he still did not have a full plot. But he had an idea for one, and that was a start.

But he did not feel like writing. He was tired from all the practice and then the stress of performing in front of a group. He knew that he would get used to doing the performances at the campfires, as he was sure that Lucy would want him to sing at all the campfires now that she had heard him.

He kicked off his boots and took off his gunbelt. But he did not have the energy to undress any further than that. He fell into his bed, hoping he'd sleep well.

But a good night's sleep was not to be for the sheriff.

Around 2AM, there was a pounding on the door to his apartment.

"Sheriff Chalmers!" a squeaky voice he recognized as Bobbie Jo. "Sheriff Chalmers! Come quick!"

Johnathan lifted his head from his pillow and looked out the window. He groaned when he saw that it was still pitch black out.

"Huh?" he grunted.

"Sheriff, please! Come quick!" she called again.

"OK," he grunted. "I'm coming."

He quickly buckled on his gunbelt and slipped into his boots. He grabbed his hat and opened the door. Bobbie Jo wrapped her arms around his waist, and he knew something was seriously wrong by how tight she squeezed.

"What is it?" he asked.

"Ghosts!"

"Ghosts?" he frowned.

"Ghosts!" she repeated. "Come on!"

He followed her downstairs and out of the office. He saw Lucy running his way. Apparently she had heard the commotion too.

"What is it?" she asked.

"Bobbie Jo says there are ghosts," he said. "Do we have regular hauntings at Camp Aldridge?"

"I mean, it is an old Western town," she shrugged. "It doesn't happen often, but there have been ghosts seen before."

"This might have been useful information to have before now," Johnathan grumbled as he and Lucy followed Bobbie Jo to the hotel she had a room in. They followed her upstairs.

In the upstairs hallway, they could see a white hazy outline of a person just as it vanished through the far wall of the building.

Johnathan wasn't quite sure what he had seen, but he knew it was not anything he wanted to see again. He stared at the spot where the apparition disappeared, willing it to stay gone.

"What, exactly, was that?" he said softly to Lucy.

"Probably someone who used to live in the town back in the time of the Old West," she shrugged. "Like I said, we see them on rare occasion, but not often."

"Well, let's make sure there are no others flying around scaring the campers," he grunted.

When they were sure the spirits were gone and all the campers were back in bed, Johnathan took Lucy back to her house before heading back to his own apartment.

The Chocolate Sheriff

CHAPTER 13

ith the campers all back in bed after the unexpected haunting, Johnathan made his way back to the Sheriff's office with the sole intent to flop into his own bed and sleep until noon.

Despite Lucy's assurance that such an event was not a common occurrence at the camp, Johnathan had the feeling that the ghosts appearing in the camp was a sign of something that was to come.

When he got back to his office and saw the old man standing by his desk, he knew for sure that the ghosts were connect to something larger.

Johnathan stopped short just inside the door to his office and stared at the old man, expecting the Native American man to disappear again as he had every time he had seen the old man.

"You stare at me as if you have seen a ghost," the old man said.

"I'm just waiting for you to disappear like you do every time I see you."

"So you have noticed me," the old man nodded. "Good. This is good."

"What is good?" The sheriff frowned. "Who are you? What are you doing in my office?"

"We have much to discuss you and I," the old man said. He sat behind the desk. "My name is John Red Crow. Miss Lucy, I know, told you of me already. I am Apache."

"You've been watching me," Johnathan crossed his arms across his chest.

"Yes," the Apache nodded.

"Why?"

"To determine the sort of man you are," John Red Crow shrugged. "To see if you are the one I have been waiting for or if there is another."

"The one you've been waiting for?" Johnathan frowned. He wasn't completely sure he liked the sound of that. "Waiting for what?"

"What Miss Lucy has built here is important," the older man said without answering Johnathan's question. "It is important that we remember our past. And it is important to give these children something special. It must be protected. That is why she has a sheriff."

"I am proud to be a part of this camp," Johnathan nodded. "It has become special to me."

"And not only because you love Miss Lucy either, I would say," John Red Crow smiled, the skin around his eyes wrinkling. He laughed when he saw Johnathan's reaction. "Oh, it's plain even to this old Apache how you feel about Miss Lucy. It is also good. You are a good person, Johnathan Chalmers. And you will be good for Lucy. I think the time will come very soon when she will be very glad you were the one she hired to become her sheriff."

"What do you mean?"

"You had visitors to the camp this evening," John Red Crow said.

Johnathan frowned. Trying to follow the Apache's line of thought was difficult. He kept meandering from topic to topic, and yet Johnathan felt as if there were only one thing on the old man's mind.

"There were some spirits that caused a stir earlier. Some of the campers were terrified."

"The spirits have told me that there are some unquiet spirits in the area," the old man nodded. "It is these unquiet spirits that visited the camp."

"What can I do to safeguard the camp and the campers from these unquiet spirits?" the sheriff asked.

"A good question," the old man nodded. "You, Johnathan Chalmers, have a gift. There is going to come a time, very quickly, when you will need it."

"What kind of gift?"

97

"I cannot tell you that," the old man said. "At least not yet. When the time comes, send for me. And I will come and help you. You will know when the time is right." The old man stood and started to walk out of the office. He stopped and turned back to face Johnathan. "I know that this is difficult for you to take on faith, Johnathan Chalmers, but you must. Know this. You are the right person in the right place at the right time."

And with that last enigmatic statement, the old man left Johnathan's office. When Johnathan went to the door to see where the old man had gone, he could not see the Apache anywhere. It was as if the old man had vanished into thin air.

CHAPTER 14

 lot of the campers were still on edge for most of the week following the haunting incident. Johnathan and the camp staff had worked extra hard to reassure the campers that they were safe.

Johnathan was trying hard not to think about what the old man had told him after the haunting. He wasn't sure what to think about what had been said. He certainly wasn't sure how much stock he put into the old man's assertion that he had some kind of spiritual gift.

He was not about to dismiss it out of hand, though. He knew that the Native Americans had a far better communion with nature and the spirit world than he did. And their shamans were the closest to that other world. No, he would be foolish to discount what John Red Crow had said. But he did not know what to do about it.

In the meantime, while he tried to figure out what that was all about, he had a pretty normal week. He gave out a lot of candy, which had made him incredibly popular with the campers. He made his rounds.

And he'd talked with Lucy about a second date.

While they had not yet set up a second date, they both agreed that there should be one. There was a definite connection between the two of them and they both could feel it. Johnathan was looking forward to exploring the relationship and seeing how far it would go. He had a feeling that she was too.

When Friday came, he jumped out of his bed, feeling suddenly nervous. He was not sure what had caused it but something was nagging at him. He just had a feeling of danger, and he did not know where it was coming from.

He did not dismiss the feeling of danger as much as he may have wanted to. Instead, he used it to keep alert. He carefully shaved, showered and dressed. As he was strapping on his gunbelt, he started to wonder what was making him feel so nervous.

As he made his way around the camp for his morning rounds, his feeling of uneasiness grew. By the time he stopped in at the general store, there was a knot in the pit of his stomach from worry.

"Hi, Sheriff," Lucy said when he walked into the store. "I'm going into Phoenix for supplies. Do you need me to pick you up anything?"

"No, thank you, Miss Lucy," he said as he walked over to the counter. "Just be careful today. I don't know what it is, but I've had a feeling of danger since I woke up this morning. Something's going on and I don't know what it is. Yet."

"I will be careful," she nodded. He felt a little better knowing she was taking his warning seriously. "You be careful too, Sheriff. It could be danger for you, too, you know."

"I know, Miss Lucy," he nodded. "But the feeling of danger is keeping me very alert."

"Good," she smiled. She leaned up and kissed his cheek. "I'll be back this afternoon and then we can discuss that second date some more. I have some ideas."

"I look forward to that," he said, blushing slightly. "Until then, Miss Lucy."

He touched the brim of his hat and went back to his rounds.

Later in the day, he was out by the saloon talking to the piano player, Penny Westin. He had not had a chance to spend much time listening to her play and he was sorry for that. From the little amount of time that he had listened to her, she was good.

He had an idea that perhaps they should be utilizing her talents far more than just her playing inside a saloon. It was something that he would have to talk to Lucy about later on.

He bade her farewell and started walking back to the general store. He stopped when he saw Bobbie Jo running up to him.

"Sheriff Johnathan, the coach is coming," she squealed. "Miss Lucy will be back soon."

"Why don't we go meet her at the station then, Bobbie Jo?" he smiled down at her.

The little girl took his hand and they walked over to the stage station. Sure enough, he could see the plume of dust in the distance that said the coach was coming. They went inside the station, and he bought her an ice cream from Roger Braddock.

"Stage was supposed to be here a half hour ago, Sheriff," Roger said. "I hope they didn't run into any trouble."

"I'm sure everything is all right," Johnathan said. "But I've been feeling like something is wrong all day, so I'll just be waiting around to make sure."

"Good," Roger nodded. "Good that you don't ignore your instincts."

They waited as they watched the stage get closer and closer to the station. When it got close enough, Johnathan frowned when he saw that the driver looked to be injured.

His sense of danger intensified.

When the coach pulled up, Tim dropped from the driver's seat and dragged himself inside.

"We were attacked," he wheezed. "Not sure by what."

"Tim, where's Miss Lucy?" Johnathan said. He'd looked in the coach, but there was no sign of her.

"I don't know," Tim groaned. "I got knocked off the coach and knocked out. When I came to, she was gone. I came back here to tell you so you can go find her."

"Roger, get Tim settled," Johnathan said softly. "I'm going back to the camp. I'll be back shortly. When I do, I'll be riding out. And I'll bring Miss Lucy back."

The Chocolate Sheriff

CHAPTER 15

hen Clive saw Johnathan running over the bridge to the camp, he came over to see what the problem was. The sheriff made his way over to the weaponsmith and leaned in close.

"Clive, Lucy is missing. I need you to do something for me," Johnathan said.

"Anything for Miss Lucy," Clive nodded.

"Go find John Red Crow and bring him here," Johnathan said. "I think I am going to need him for this."

"Right away," Clive nodded.

Johnathan watched as Clive ran off. He knew the other man would be back quickly.

They all loved Lucy, even if not the same way that Johnathan was starting to, and the fact that she was missing was disturbing to all of them.

They would all do everything they could to find her. But it was on Johnathan to do so.

He was the sheriff after all.

It did not take long for Clive to return with the old Apache man. Johnathan had a feeling that John Red Crow had been expecting Clive. Or, if not Clive, he'd been expecting someone.

"Here he is, Sheriff Johnathan," Clive said.

"Thanks, Clive," Johnathan said, clapping his friend on the shoulder.

"There is trouble?" the old Apache asked. The look on his face told Johnathan he already knew the answer to the question.

"Miss Lucy is missing," Johnathan said quietly. "I suspect that this is the trouble you warned me about."

"You are correct," John Red Crow nodded. "It is time."

"Can you track her from where the coach was attacked?" the sheriff asked.

"Probably," the Apache said. "Better than you can, I would think."

"Considering I know next to nothing about tracking, I would say that's a good bet," Johnathan grimaced. "We're going to ride out now. I don't want to waste any more time."

"I am ready," the old man nodded.

Johnathan nodded in thanks and led the way back across the bridge to the stage coach station. The Apache followed quietly behind him. They were both silent as they walked to the station.   Johnathan was lost in worry about Lucy.   John Red Crow was content to let the younger man be lost in thought.

When they got to the station, Johnathan went over to the counter to talk to Roger Braddock.

"Was Tim able to tell you where they were attacked?" Johnathan asked.

"About halfway between here and Phoenix," Roger said. "He said that you should be able to see where he fell out of the coach."

"He might be able to," Johnathan said, pointing to John Red Crow. "I'm pretty sure I won't be able to."

"Good thing you're bringing a Native American with you, then," Roger nodded. "Smart of you."

"I was always taught that if you did not know something, you should seek out someone who does," Johnathan shrugged. "He knows what I don't."

"About a great many things," John Red Crow added softly.

Roger chuckled softly.   "Your stallion is ready, and I have a good mare you can borrow, sir."

"Thank you," the Apache nodded.

"Good hunting," Roger said. "Bring her back safely."

"We will," Johnathan nodded.

The sheriff led the way out to the horses and mounted up.   They rode off in the direction of Phoenix.

About thirty minutes of hard riding brought them to where the coach had been attacked. They stopped the horses and dismounted.

John Red Crow made his way around the scene of the attack, looking at the ground very carefully. After what seemed like hours, he stopped and looked off to the distance.

"This way," he said. "Lead the horses. We'll walk. It will be easier to follow her steps that way."

"OK," Johnathan nodded.

They walked for another half hour. The Apache kept watching the ground in front of him for signs of Lucy's footsteps. He was careful to make sure that Johnathan followed close behind. He did not want to have to go looking for the younger man.

Soon enough, they saw what looked like someone lying on the ground in the distance.

They picked up the pace, knowing time was of the essence. When they got there, they saw that it was, in fact, Lucy lying on the ground.

She wasn't moving.

CHAPTER 16

Johnathan took a deep breath to calm himself so that he would not panic. The sight of the woman he had come to love lying lifeless on the ground was enough to induce a large amount of panic in him. But he knew that he would do no good for her if he panicked.

And right now, he knew, he was the only hope that she had to make it through.

He knelt down next to her and checked for a pulse. She had a very faint pulse, so he knew she was still alive. She was barely breathing, though, and he knew he would need to do something and soon if he was going to save her life. He was not sure how, though.

109

"What's wrong with her?" Johnathan asked in a quiet voice.

"An unquiet spirit has taken over her body," the old man said after a few moments with his eyes closed. "Her spirit is locked in battle with the unquiet spirit. There is nothing I can do for her." He looked up at Johnathan, his gaze piercing deep into Johnathan's soul. "But there is something you can."

"What can I do that you can't?" the sheriff asked.

"You can pull the unquiet spirit from her," the old man said. "I will guide you."

"Anything," Johnathan nodded. "So long as she is safe."

"There is no guarantee of that, Johnathan Chalmers," the old man sighed. "It is up to her to wake once the unquiet spirit has left her body. She may not."

"What must I do?"

"First, you must quiet your center," the old man said. "You cannot help her if your core is unquiet. You will end up the same as her if you try to draw off the unquiet spirit as you are now."

"Calm my center," he grimaced. "Easier said than done when the woman I love is lying there close to death."

"If you love her as you claim, then you will do this thing," the old man admonished. "Take deep breaths and close your eyes. You will know when your center is calm."

Johnathan closed his eyes and took several long deep breaths. It took several long minutes, but he could feel his center starting to loosen and relax. Finally he could feel that he was completely calm. Even then, he took several more deep breaths before opening his eyes.

When he did, he could see a light haze over John Red Crow. When he looked down at Lucy, he frowned. He could see two different and competing auras surrounding the young woman. One was a soft warm yellow. He associated that with Lucy. The warmth of the yellow reminded him of Lucy's warmth and generosity when it came to the campers.

The other aura was an angry red. He knew that was the unquiet spirit that had tried to take over Lucy's body.

He kept himself calm while he studied the second aura. He knew that the red aura needed to be removed. It was overlapping Lucy's yellow aura, and he knew that if something did not happen soon, the red aura would completely over take her aura and she would be lost.

He could not let that happen.

"I see two different auras inside her," he said slowly.

"You must draw the unquiet spirit out of her body and into your own," the old man said. "Blow into her mouth as if you were helping her breath. The unquiet spirit will enter your body that way."

Johnathan nodded and bent over Lucy. Gently, he pinched her nose and tilted her head like he was giving her mouth to mouth resuscitation. He leaned down and blew into her mouth.

When he touched his mouth to hers, he could feel a searing heat entering his throat. He pulled away from Lucy, pulling the unquiet spirit with him. When he was sure he had the entire spirit, he stood up and walked several feet away from her.

He turned away from Lucy and exhaled deeply, expelling the spirit from his own body forcefully. He could see the red aura twisting away from them.

When the spirit was gone, he turned back to Lucy and knelt back down.

"The spirit is gone," John Red Crow said. "It is up to Lucy to wake up on her own."

"Let's get her to the hospital in Phoenix," he said. "Maybe there is something that they can do."

Johnathan carried Lucy over to his horse and hoisted her up over the saddle. He held her there while he climbed up in the saddle. He wrapped an arm around her middle and held her tight against him so that she would not fall off the saddle while they rode the rest of the way into Phoenix. John Red Crow followed close behind him.

It was all Johnathan could do to keep her safe while he got her to the hospital. He was determined not to lose her now that they had fallen for each other.

CHAPTER 17

he hospital they had taken Lucy to was always busy. It was, from all that Johnathan could tell, a very good hospital though. That was good, as far as he was concerned. He would not have wanted her case handled by anyone but the best.

As he had been since he and John Red Crow brought Lucy in, Johnathan Chalmers sat by her bedside. The doctor had given Lucy a complete workup when they'd brought her in. He was waiting for the doctor to come back in with some kind of news.

He was holding her hand gently, hoping that the love and care he was showing her would help her come back. He was prepared to keep Camp Aldridge going without her. What they were doing for the kids was too important to end if she were to not make it.

But it would be better still if she were to remain at the helm.

And so, Johnathan sat by her bedside waiting for her to awaken.

He had sent John Red Crow back to the camp to let the rest of the staff know what had happened. It was bad enough that the camp would be without Lucy for however long she was going to be laid up. But Johnathan was going to be splitting his time between the hospital and the camp. As much as his duty was to keep the camp safe, he felt that he also had the duty to look after the leader of that camp.

He would have felt that way even if he did not love her.

He had started to doze slightly when the door to Lucy's hospital room opened. Startled, he looked up to see the doctor walking in. He looked over at Lucy and then turned back to the doctor, still holding her hand.

"What can you tell me, Doctor?" he asked in a hushed voice.

"Well, whatever happened to her caused some severe brain trauma," the doctor began. "I can't tell you exactly how severe it really is, but that is the reason she hasn't woken up."

"Will be she all right?"

"I honestly can't answer that question," the doctor sighed. "The brain is a funny thing. She's going to have to find a reason to wake up. Or her brain could just decide that the pain is too much and she'll never wake up."

"But if she does?"

"If she wakes up, I believe she will be fine," the doctor said. "But with a trauma like this where I can't even assess how bad the damage is, I just don't know. You probably should prepare for her to never wake."

"She'll wake," Johnathan said. "She's strong and she has a lot to live for with her camp."

"I hope you're right," the doctor nodded. "I'll be back to check on her later on."

Johnathan nodded before turning back to watch Lucy, saying a silent prayer that she'd wake.

Three days later, Johnathan was back by Lucy's bedside. He had spent most of the day at the camp, making sure things were running smoothly without Lucy. The campers were all sad that she had been injured and wanted to know when Miss Lucy would be back.

All Johnathan could tell them was he hoped she'd be back soon.

And so, as soon as the campers had assembled in the dining hall for dinner, Johnathan had gotten on his stallion and galloped out of Camp Aldridge, heading for Phoenix so he could spend the evening by her side.

When he got to the hospital, he checked in at the nurses' station for the unit her room was in, where he was told there had been no change. It was not what he had wanted to hear even though he had expected as much.

He went into her room. The nurses had all seen him there, and they all knew that he would sit by her bedside until the wee hours of the morning before he would go back to the camp. They respected his dedication to her, even if some of them found the situation sad. Nurses always felt bad when someone as young as Lucy was cut down. All they could do was keep giving her the best care they could and hope she came out of it.

He sat by her bedside, gently holding her hand as he did every night. Tears leaked from his eyes as he watched her labored breathing. He wished that he could do something for her. But he knew that there was nothing he could do but to watch and wait.

"Come on, Lucy," he whispered. "Come back to us. The camp needs you. I need you."

He watched her face for any change. There was none, much as there had been no change at all in the three nights previous. It did not change the fact that he was hopeful that there would one day be a change.

"Come back to me, Lucy," he said, tears causing his voice to shake. He bowed his head over their linked hands and let a couple tears fall from his eyes. "I love you."

"I... love you, too," Lucy's voice came back, albeit very weakly.

116

His eyes snapped up to her face, shocked that she had responded. Lucy's bright green eyes were open and she was watching him. It was clear she was still very weak, but she was alive and she was awake.

He gave her hand a gentle squeeze, which made her lips twitch upward in what might have become a full smile had she not suddenly been overcome by a fit of coughing.

Johnathan got her to sit up so that she could breathe easier and then reached up and pressed the nurse call button.

"Thanks," she said, her voice barely above a whisper. "Johnathan, where am I?"

"You're in the hospital, Miss Lucy," he said. "This is your fourth night here. Do you remember anything?"

"Water, please," she whispered. He poured a glass of water and handed it to her. She took a tentative sip before continuing. "The last thing I remember is leaving the camp to pick up supplies. Something must have happened."

Before he could tell her anything, the nurse rushed into the room to answer the call button. She skidded to a stop when she saw Lucy sitting up in bed and awake.

"Well, this is a pleasantly surprising change," the nurse smiled broadly. "How are you feeling, Miss McCullors?"

"Like I've been run over by my stagecoach," Lucy croaked. "But I'm alive."

"You have this man to thank for that," the nurse said. Lucy looked at Johnathan and finally did smile. "He brought you in. You were in bad shape. We weren't sure you'd pull through. He never doubted you would though."

"Have you been sitting here this entire time, Johnathan?" she asked.

"Not the entire time, no," he shook his head. "I spent my days at the camp making sure that it was running smoothly without us there. We have excellent coworkers, though, and the camp is doing just fine. At night, I'd come here and sit by your side. I hoped that having someone nearby who cared about you would help bring you back."

"You were right," she said. She took another sip of her water. "Thank you, Johnathan."

"The doctor will want to look you over in the morning, Miss McCullors," the nurse said. 'You've been through quite an ordeal. I am sure you will be our guest for a few days yet while he makes sure you will recover fully."

"Don't worry about the camp, Miss Lucy," Johnathan said. "We can get by for another few days. The campers will be very happy to have you back though. There are a great many people at the camp who love you, you know."

"Including my Chocolate Sheriff, it would seem," Lucy smiled, a twinkle returning to her eyes.

It was a good sign, Johnathan decided. He knew that Lucy was on the mend.

After the nurse left, Johnathan explained what happened and how he had come to find her and save her. Lucy just listened, nodding to keep him going. When he was done, she sighed.

"It hardly seems believable," she said. "But yet here I am in the hospital. And you saved me."

"I couldn't sit by and do nothing," he squeezed her hand. "You hired me to be the sheriff. That includes protecting you, Miss Lucy."

"So it would seem."

They talked for another few minutes before she lay back in the bed to sleep again. But he knew that the worst was over and that Lucy was going to be fine. He leaned up and kissed her on the forehead.

Then he sat back in the chair by her bed, sighing with relief.

The Chocolate Sheriff

CHAPTER 18

It had been four days since Lucy had returned to the camp from the hospital. In that time, Johnathan had been making sure that she was taking things easy. It was not easy to get Lucy to slow down, but the doctor had been insistent that she needed to take things slow while she healed up from her ordeal. And Johnathan was there to make sure she followed the doctor's orders.

The campers had all been happy when Miss Lucy had returned to Camp Aldridge. As the owner of the camp, Lucy was well loved by the campers, and they all had been upset when she had been hurt. Johnathan's reputation had gone way up in the camper's eyes for the way he rescued her.

The campers had spread whispered rumors that Sheriff Johnathan was in love with Miss Lucy. Many of the campers expected that the two would one day marry.

It was something that the campers were hoping for, as they felt that Miss Lucy and the Chocolate Sheriff deserved some happiness in their lives. After all, they devoted their lives to bringing happiness to the campers' lives.

Johnathan had had more than one camper come up to him and express a desire for him to propose to Miss Lucy. It made him smile inside every time he heard it, but he did not let on that he had been planning on doing so ever since she had been hurt. He'd known from the moment that he'd seen her lying on the ground that he could not live his life without her. It was what had made him able to save her.

And so, while she was in the hospital, Johnathan had begun to plan.

It was a beautiful Friday morning, and Johnathan was in a good mood. But he was nervous. He would be proposing to Lucy that evening. Of course, he had no way of knowing what she would say, but he hoped she was going to say yes. He had a feeling that she was going to, which made it easier. The two of them had clicked from the first, and it only made sense for them to take this next step.

There was only one problem with his plan. He had ordered the ring for the proposal, but it had yet to arrive. He would go through with the proposal without the ring if he had to, but he really hoped it would be in the mail.

He stepped into the general store to pick up a couple of things for his evening plans. He had planned a lovely picnic on the hill overlooking the camp. Lucy loved simple things like that, he knew, and he could not think of a better place for him to pop the question.

"Hey, Miss Libbie," he said as he got up to the counter. "Is there, by chance, mail for your favorite sheriff today?"

"There sure is, Sheriff," she smiled at him. She bent over and retrieved a small box from under the counter. "Is this what I think it is?"

"I suppose that all depends on what you think it is," he shrugged as he picked up the box.

"I think that it is a ring for Miss Lucy," Libbie winked at him. "A diamond ring."

"Well don't tell her! I want it to be a surprise!" Johnathan laughed. "I have a lovely picnic planned for her tonight."

"Sheriff, I believe you will find that your plan to propose to Miss Lucy may well be the worst kept secret in Camp Aldridge," Libbie laughed harder. "I dare say Miss Lucy knows it's coming."

"Do you have any idea what she might say when I ask?"

"Well, I can't say for sure, but I do believe you will be happy with her answer," Libbie said. "We girls talk, you know. She'd never tell you herself, but she has heard the whispers among the campers, and she does hope that the rumors are true."

"Well, that does easy my nerves a little," Johnathan nodded. He touched the brim of his hat, dipping it just a bit in Libbie's direction. "Thank you for the supplies, Miss Libbie. I am sure that you'll hear about tonight soon enough."

"Go get her, Sheriff!"

Later that day, Johnathan climbed up in the saddle of his silver stallion and rode his way over to Lucy's house. When he got there, he slid off the saddle and went to knock on the door. She opened the door just as he was getting ready to knock and gave him a bright smile.

"Johnathan, what a pleasant surprise!" she said. "Would you like to come in?"

"Actually, Miss Lucy, I came to see if you were feeling well enough for a leisurely ride out to the hills overlooking the camp. It's a pretty night for a picnic, and I thought you could use a lovely evening out."

"Why, Sheriff! That sounds quite lovely. Let me get my hat, and we can go."

It wasn't long before Lucy came out of her house, her straw sun hat perched jauntily on her head. She leaned up on her tippy toes and planted a quick peck on his cheek. He smiled down at her and helped her mount the horse. When he saw that she was secure on the saddle, he swung himself up behind her on the stallion. He put an arm around her to keep her on the saddle then clicked at the horse to get him to start slowly walking.

They took it easy, a slow trot out of the camp and up the trail to a nice flat grassy spot on a hill overlooking Camp Aldridge.

Johnathan swung his leg over the saddle and dropped to the ground. He helped Lucy down, causing her to smile at him again. He hobbled the horse, making sure that the stallion was in a location where he had plenty of grass to graze on. Johnathan pulled the blanket and basket off the saddle. Lucy helped him spread the blanket flat on the ground. She sat on the blanket while he spread out the food he had brought. When he sat right next to her on the blanket, her smile widened.

"This is lovely, Johnathan," she said as she leaned up against him. "It is a lovely night for a picnic. And you're right. I did need this."

"You've had a rough week, Miss Lucy," he shrugged as he put his arm around her. "I just thought I would do something nice for you."

"What a wonderfully thoughtful gesture," she said as she snuggled closer. "And everything looks so good too."

They ate in silence, simply enjoying each other's company while they watched the sun slowly sink in the distance. It was a beautiful night with clear skies, and the temperature was neither too hot nor too cold. It was a perfect early fall evening, and they enjoyed sitting in each other's arms. Neither of them got to slow down much while at the camp, so an evening stolen away like this was a luxury they both cherished.

When they had finish eating, Johnathan pulled very slightly away from Lucy and turned to face her. It was the moment he had been waiting for, and the moment could not have been more perfect had he planned it.

"Miss Lucy, I have to admit, I had an ulterior motive for having you come out here with me tonight," he said softly.

"You mean, this wasn't just to get me away from the camp for a few hours?" she asked with a twinkle in her eye.

"Well, yes, that was part of why I brought you out here, but it isn't the only reason," he stammered.

"You don't have any nefarious plans for my honor, do you?" Somehow, she managed to keep a   straight   face.
"No, it's nothing like that, Miss Lucy!" He pulled back, shocked that she would even ask. "I just.... There's something I want to say to you."

"I know." "You know?"

"Johnathan, everyone knows," she laughed. "How you feel about me is not exactly the best kept secret in the camp, you know."

"I was hoping this was going to be more of a surprise," he said with a sad note in his voice.

"So, do you have something to ask me?" she asked. She couldn't keep torturing him. It wasn't fair to him to do so. Better to have him just get the question out in the open so she could answer him.

"Miss Lucy, when I saw you lying there not breathing, it made me realize just how much I have come to care for you," he said. "It's not just the job and the chance you took on me. You are a genuinely amazing person. Just look at what you have done by putting Camp Aldridge together. I mean, it is incredible what you have been able to do for these kids. I am honored to be a part of that."

"I could not imagine doing anything else," she shrugged. "What we give those kids is a once in a lifetime opportunity that they will never forget. And I am glad that you have become a part of it too, Johnathan."

He smiled at her as he pulled a small box out of his inside vest pocket. Nervously and gently, he opened the box and set it on the ground in front of her.

"What I realized when I saw you lying there was that I did not want to live the rest of my life without you," he continued. "And so, Miss Lucy, I want to ask you... Will you marry me?"

Lucy picked up the ring and looked at it. Without a word, she slipped it onto her finger.

"Is that a yes?"

"Of course it's a yes," she laughed. She leaned up and gently touched her lips to his. "Did you honestly think there would be any other answer?"

"Well, I was hopeful, but I did not know for sure!"

She laughed again and then leaned back against him, letting him wrap his arms back around her.

They sat like that until long after the sun had slipped from the sky entirely.

EPILOGUE

ell, there you have it, Faithful Readers. That was the story of the Chocolate Sheriff. I know it's a difficult story to believe. That's why I checked into Johnathan's tale before I agreed to bring it to you.

I am thankful that Johnathan and Lucy have trusted me to tell their story to the world. I can only hope I have done the story justice.

As for what happened to Johnathan and Lucy after the events I've chronicled in this book... Well, they did go on to get married. I was at their wedding this past June. It was a lovely ceremony. The night before the wedding, the three of us sat down in my hotel room, and I showed them the first draft of the manuscript I had done for this book. You see, I had wanted their approval before I even sent the manuscript off to my editor, let alone the publisher. It was their story after all.

They enjoyed how I told the tale. I think they were surprised at how little embellishment I put on what they'd told me. But why would I embellish such a wonderful and touching tale?

When you are handed the perfect story, you tell it just as it is.

And so, my Faithful Readers, I hope you have enjoyed their tale. Every word I wrote in these pages happened just as I wrote it. It is up to each of you to believe it or not.

I know I do.

Someday, I will go back out to Arizona for a promotional tour. When I do, I will check in with Johnathan and Lucy.

I hope that they will have another story for me...

-Rick Bentsen
October 3, 2016

ABOUT THE AUTHOR

Rick Bentsen released his first novel in 2001. It was a simple science fiction story that was somewhat well received. Although it never sold very well, the people that read his first novel enjoyed it immensely. From that first moment, Rick was hooked.

Rick has long loved science fiction and fantasy books and movies and that love has turned into a writing passion. He has recently added a mystery/thriller series to his normal science fiction and fantasy series as projects to complete.

Rick lives in southeastern Massachusetts which he believes is the most beautiful place in the world. Fall in New England, he finds to be the most inspirational time of the year with all the colors.

Rick can be reached through his facebook page on which he regularly talks about his writing, cats, and coffee. (www.facebook.com/RickBentsenAuthor)